Dirty Bertie
MONSTER!

DAVID ROBERTS WRITTEN BY ALAN MACDONALD

Stripes

Collect all the
Dirty Bertie books!

Dirty Bertie

MONSTER!

To Joel ~ D R

For my dear Sally x ~ A M

STRIPES PUBLISHING
An imprint of the Little Tiger Group
1 The Coda Centre, 189 Munster Road,
London SW6 6AW

A paperback original
First published in Great Britain in 2016

Characters created by David Roberts
Text copyright © Alan MacDonald, 2016
Illustrations copyright © David Roberts, 2016

ISBN: 978-1-84715-725-6

Contents

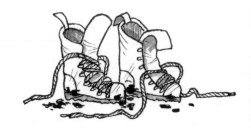

MONSTER!

CHAPTER 1

Miss Boot glared at her class, waiting for silence.

"The Summer Fair is only a week away, and I need polite, sensible children to help run the stalls," she said. Her eyes fell on Bertie, who was drawing on the back of his hand. She sighed – he was about as sensible as a fruit bat.

Dirty Bertie

Bertie put down his felt-tip pen and sat forward. There was only one stall he and his friends were interested in running, and he hoped that no one else pinched it.

"I've made a list of all the stalls," said Miss Boot. "Raise your hand if you would like to help with one of them. First, the book stall…"

Bertie waited as Miss Boot worked her way down the list.

"Next, face painting," she said.

Bertie's hand flew into the air. Darren and Eugene leaped out of their seats excitedly.

"Ooh! Ooh, Miss! Can we do it? Can we?" they begged.

"We'd be brilliant at face painting," said Bertie.

Miss Boot sucked in her breath. She imagined entrusting Bertie with a set of face paints. He'd probably give people revolting spots or ugly warts. In no time there'd be a queue of wailing children and angry parents demanding their money back. It was out of the question.

"I don't think that's a good idea," she said. "Donna and Pamela, I'm sure I could rely on you."

"But what about us?" moaned Bertie.

Dirty Bertie

"I have another job for you," said Miss Boot. "The Lucky Dip – you can't do any damage with that."

THE LUCKY DIP? NO! Bertie slumped back in his seat. Why did they always get the most boring stall at the fair? There was nothing to do on the Lucky Dip, and the prizes were rubbish. Last year Bertie had won a bar of scented soap – what was "lucky" about that? Besides, he was brilliant at face painting.

When the bell rang for break, Bertie trailed outside with his friends.

"It's not fair," he complained. "We never get chosen for anything!"

"The Lucky Dip… BOR-ING!" groaned Darren.

Dirty Bertie

"Well, there's nothing we can do. Miss Boot won't change her mind," sighed Eugene.

"We're not beaten yet," said Bertie.

He'd set his heart on face painting and he wasn't giving up without a fight. After all, anything could happen on the day. With a bit of luck, Donna and Pamela might be allergic to face paints.

CHAPTER 2

The day of the Summer Fair arrived.
Miss Boot stood at the school gates,
greeting people as they came in. The
sun was shining and the school field was
packed with visitors. Everyone seemed
to be having fun – everyone except
Bertie and his friends at the Lucky Dip.

Bertie sat kicking his feet behind a

large black bin filled with sawdust.

"LUCKY DIP – A PRIZE EVERY
TIME!" said the sign. So far they'd only
had two customers – one had won a
plastic key ring and the other a jar of
elastic bands.

"This is rubbish," grumbled Darren.

Bertie gazed longingly at the face-
painting stall, where a queue of children
waited their turn. Donna was painting
someone as a mermaid while Pamela
drew a butterfly on a toddler's cheek.

"Look at that," said Bertie
in disgust. "They're
not even doing it
properly!"

"Maybe we could
ask them to swap?"
suggested Eugene.

"Fat chance!" snorted Darren. "Who wants to run the Lucky Dip? The prizes are all useless!"

Suddenly Bertie had an idea. What if the Lucky Dip prizes weren't so useless? What if it was a gold mine and everyone wanted a go? Then Donna and Pamela might be tempted to swap with them!

"Lend me a pound, Eugene," said Bertie.

"What?"

"Come on," said Bertie. "Do you want to do face painting or not?"

Reluctantly Eugene handed over one of the coins he'd brought for the fair. Bertie wrapped the coin in red tissue paper and hid it near the top of the bin.

A few minutes later Royston Rich stopped at the stall.

Dirty Bertie

"Lucky Dip – a prize every time!"
cried Bertie. "Try your luck, Royston!"

Royston handed over his money and
plunged his hand into the sawdust.

"The best prizes are near the top,"
Bertie whispered.

Dirty Bertie

Royston pulled out a ball of red tissue paper. He unwrapped it to reveal Eugene's shiny pound coin.

"WOW! I won a pound!" he cried.

"That's nothing," said Bertie. "Don't tell anyone, but there's a fortune in here — maybe a hundred pounds!"

"Never!" gasped Royston.

"Don't say I told you," whispered Bertie.

Royston quickly paid for another go.
This time he won a pencil sharpener,
but it didn't put him off. He rushed off
to tell his friends.

"ONE HUNDRED POUNDS?" cried
Darren. "You made that up!"

"Of course I did, but Royston doesn't
know that," said Bertie. "You wait, soon
everyone will want a go. Then we'll see
if Donna and Pamela want to swap."

Bertie was right. Once word got around
that the Lucky Dip was a treasure trove,
it began to draw a crowd. Children
queued in the hope of finding a five or
ten pound note. Eventually Donna and
Pamela came over to see what the fuss
was about.

Dirty Bertie

"What's going on?" asked Pamela.

"Royston won a pound," Bertie explained. "It turns out the Lucky Dip's full of money."

"Really?" said Donna.

"Yes, we've won quite a bit ourselves," said Bertie. "Haven't we Eugene?"

Dirty Bertie

"Oh ... er, yes, we have," said Eugene.

"Millions!" said Darren.

"Wow!" said Pamela. "I wish Miss Boot had given us the Lucky Dip!"

Bertie pretended to consider. "Well, I suppose we could swap stalls for a bit," he offered generously.

Pamela and Donna looked at each other.

"Could we?" asked Donna. "But what about Miss Boot?"

"She won't care!" said Bertie. "She's too busy to notice."

"Okay, you're on," said Pamela.

Bertie smiled to himself. *At last!* he thought. Now was his chance to show what could really be done with a set of face paints!

CHAPTER 3

"This is wicked," said Darren. "I just turned Royston Rich into a rat!"

"And I gave Angela Nicely measles," said Eugene. "She loved it!"

Bertie and his friends had been busy. So far they hadn't painted any mermaids, fairies or butterflies – instead they had done two pirates, a werewolf and a ghost.

Dirty Bertie

Bertie nudged Darren. "Look, there's Know-All Nick," he said. "Let's paint him."

"Yes," grinned Darren. "We could make him really UGLY."

"He's ugly already," said Eugene.

Know-All Nick caught sight of the stall and stopped.

"Face painting?" he smirked. "I thought Miss Boot put you on the Lucky Dip."

"She did, but we swapped," said Bertie. "Why don't we paint you, Nick?"

"No thanks," replied Nick. "My mum says I've got sensitive skin."

"It's okay, these are extra-sensitive face paints," said Bertie.

"I bet you'd look great with your face painted," said Darren.

"You think so?" said Nick.

"Oh yes, with a face like yours you could be anything," said Eugene. "A superhero, for instance."

Nick's eyes lit up. Secretly he'd always believed he'd make a fantastic superhero. He could be TIDYMAN – saving the world from smelly socks and pants.

Dirty Bertie

He narrowed his eyes. "But how do I know you won't play a trick on me?" he asked.

"US?" said Bertie. "As if we'd do that!"

"So what's it to be?" asked Darren. "A wizard or a superhero?"

Nick shook his head. "Make me a lion," he said. "A big scary lion."

Bertie raised his eyebrows. He couldn't think of anyone *less* like a lion than Nick – he was more of a slug or a worm. In any case, a lion wasn't much of a challenge. Nick deserved something better, something special. Wait, he had it – the perfect idea. People would certainly get a fright when they saw Nick's face. Bertie whispered to his friends, who grinned and nodded.

"What are you saying?" whined Nick.

"Nothing!" said Bertie. "We'll make you a lion. Close your eyes so you don't get paint in them."

Nick sat down and did as he was told.

"Right, let's get started," said Bertie. He reached for the green and daubed it all over Nick's face.

"What are you doing?" demanded Nick.

"Just putting on the base colour," replied Bertie. "Golden for a lion."

"Don't forget the whiskers," said Nick.

"Don't worry," said Bertie. "I won't."

He reached for another face paint and gave Nick thick black eyebrows. Next he added ugly scars running across his forehead.

"Do I look like a lion?" asked Nick.

"Definitely," grinned Eugene. "A *monster* lion."

Finally Bertie wet Nick's hair and
shaped it into jagged peaks.

"This is your lion's mane," he said.
"There we are – finished!"

He stood back to admire his work.

"Oh, yes!" said Eugene. "The Lion King!"

"Dead scary!" said Darren.

Nick stood up. Bertie had thought
Nick was ugly before, but now he made

Dracula seem handsome.

"Where's the mirror? I want to see myself!" cried Nick.

"Oh, um, sorry, Darren broke the mirror," said Bertie, hiding it behind his back.

"But we promise you won't be disappointed," said Darren.

Dirty Bertie

Nick showed his claws. "Am I really scary?" he asked.

"Very scary," said Bertie. "Why don't you creep up on someone and give them a fright?"

"I'm going to!" said Nick. "You watch, I'm going to creep up and roar. GRRRR!"

"Oh, help, help! It's a lion!" whimpered Bertie. "That'll be fifty pence, please."

Nick paid and went off looking pleased with his new look.

Eugene laughed. "He's not going to be too happy when he sees himself."

"No, not when he finds out he looks like Frankenstein's monster," said Darren.

"Well, if you ask me, I think it's a big improvement," said Bertie.

CHAPTER 4

Nick made his way through the crowds.
People turned to stare as he went past.
A toddler saw him and burst into tears.

*Anyone would think they'd never seen a
lion before!* thought Nick. He practised
his roar under his breath. "ROOARR!"

Who should he sneak up on first?
Trevor or maybe Royston Rich? No,

they'd both pretend they weren't scared.
What he wanted was someone who'd
really scream with fright. Come to think
of it, his mum could scream quite loudly.
He spotted her at the refreshment stall,
chatting with Miss Boot over a cup of tea.

Perfect, thought Nick. *Wait till a lion
creeps up and pounces on them.*

Back at their stall, Bertie and his friends
watched as Nick slunk over to the
refreshment stall and dropped down on
all fours.

"What's he doing now?" asked Eugene.

"Pretending to be a lion," said Darren.

"Maybe he's creeping up on someone,"
said Bertie. "Wait, isn't that Miss Boot?"

"Yes," said Eugene. "And she's talking

Dirty Bertie

to Nick's mum."

Surely Nick wasn't planning to scare his mum and Miss Boot?

"Come on!" said Bertie, hurrying over. "I wouldn't miss this for anything."

As they reached the refreshment stall, they were just in time to see Nick crawl under his mum's table.

"I'm so glad Nicholas is doing well," Nick's mum was saying. "He's such a kind and sensible boy…"

Bertie saw a hand grip the table. Then a ghastly green face rose up above a plate of cupcakes. Miss Boot turned her head and gasped, dropping her teacup.

Dirty Bertie

"GRAAAARR!" roared Nick.

"EEEK!" screamed his mum, falling backwards off her chair.

Know-All Nick jumped out, growling and showing his teeth.

"GRRRR! GRAAAARR!"

Miss Boot stared at the monster. She knew that face.

"NICHOLAS!" she thundered. "IS THIS YOUR IDEA OF A JOKE?"

"Did I scare you?" cried Know-All Nick.

"Good heavens, Nicholas! What have you done to your face?" gasped his mum.

"It's face paint," said Nick. "I'm a lion! GRRRR!"

"A lion indeed!" snorted Miss Boot. "I've never heard such nonsense. Take a look at yourself!"

She grabbed her handbag and brought out a pocket mirror. Nick stared at his reflection in horror.

"But … I look like FRANKENSTEIN'S MONSTER!" he wailed.

"Yes," said Miss Boot. "I'm surprised at you, Nicholas. And Donna and Pamela should be ashamed."

"But it wasn't Donna and Pamela," moaned Nick. "It was Bertie! He tricked me! He said I was a big scary lion."

"BERTIE?" barked Miss Boot. "I warned

him to keep away from the face paints!
Where is that wretched boy?"

She looked around. But there was no
sign of Bertie or his friends – not at the
face-painting stall or anywhere else.

Bertie had heard Miss Boot bawl his
name and had legged it back to the
Lucky Dip to hide. He peeped out of
the bin. All in all, the Summer Fair hadn't
turned out so badly. He was looking
forward to seeing Know-All Nick on
Monday. Perhaps from now on they
should just call him Nickenstein…

BUSKERS!

CHAPTER 1

It was Saturday morning and Bertie was out shopping with Mum and Suzy. He couldn't see the point of shopping, unless it involved sweets or toys. Today, however, Suzy needed new school shoes. He trailed behind them along the high street. *Is anything more boring than shoe shopping?* he thought.

Dirty Bertie

The sound of music drifted down the street. Outside a shop, a man was tootling away on some sort of instrument. Bertie stopped in his tracks.

"It's just a busker," said Mum. "Come on, Bertie, we don't have time."

Dirty Bertie

Bertie didn't hear — he had already wandered over to take a closer look.

BOOM, CHIKKA, BOOM!

The busker had a drum machine tapping out a tinny rhythm.

But something else had caught Bertie's eye. Lying on the pavement was a hat — a hat full of money! As Bertie stared, someone dropped fifty pence into the hat as they went by. Bertie could hardly believe it. He'd seen people throw coins in a fountain, but never a hat before! Perhaps it was a lucky hat? He stooped down to pick it up.

"Look at this!" he called to Suzy.

The music came to a sudden halt.

"Hey, you! Get your thieving hands off!" cried the busker.

Mum came running over.

"What are you doing?" she hissed, snatching the hat from Bertie.

"I'm so sorry," she said, handing it back to the busker. "I'm sure he wasn't going to keep it."

"Why not?" asked Bertie. "It was just lying there!"

Mum grabbed Bertie by the arm and marched him off.

Dirty Bertie

"What?" said Bertie. "I was only looking at it!"

Suzy rolled her eyes. "You are *so* embarrassing," she groaned.

At the shoe shop, Bertie fidgeted while Suzy tried on endless pairs of shoes.

"How was I to know the hat was his?" he grumbled.

"Why do you think he left it there?" asked Mum.

"Don't ask me," said Bertie. "It's a stupid place to leave a hat!"

"It's there to collect the money!" explained Mum. "Buskers play on the street. If you like the music then you drop money in their hat."

"What? Just for blowing a trumpet?"

said Bertie.

"It was a saxophone," sighed Suzy. "And actually he was pretty good."

Bertie stared. Wait a minute… So you could play music on the street and people would actually pay you? Why hadn't someone told him this before?

"Can anyone do busking?" he asked.

"No, you have to be able to play an instrument," said Suzy.

"I can play," said Bertie. "I used to play the recorder."

"Yes, until you broke it," said Mum.

"Well, I bet I could play the saxophone," said Bertie. "Our music teacher says I must be good at something."

"Whatever she says, you're not going busking," said Mum firmly.

Dirty Bertie

"Why not?" asked Bertie.

"Because you're way too young!" said Mum.

Bertie sighed. He didn't see what his age had got to do with it. He bet Darren and Eugene wouldn't think he was too young. Come to think of it, why didn't they all go busking together? With three of them they could make an almighty racket! They were bound to earn a fortune!

CHAPTER 2

The shopping trip was a failure. Suzy couldn't find any school shoes she liked and by eleven o'clock they were back home. Bertie rang Darren and Eugene and invited them round, eager to tell them his latest idea.

"BUSKING?" said Darren. "You must be joking!"

Dirty Bertie

"Why not?" said Bertie. "All you do is put down a hat and people give you money. It's easy!"

"Yes, if you're a busker," said Eugene.

"We don't even play instruments," Darren pointed out.

"We do," argued Bertie. "Eugene plays the violin."

"I'm *learning* the violin," Eugene corrected him. "I've only had a few lessons."

"And who's going to pay to listen to us?" asked Darren.

"Loads of people," said Bertie. "You could play the drums and I can sing and play my kazoo."

Bertie had got a plastic kazoo in his Christmas stocking. It was easy to play – you just had to blow and hum at the same time. For a few weeks he'd driven his family up the wall.

"Anyway, we don't know any songs," said Eugene.

"That's why we're going to practise," said Bertie. "You fetch your violin and I'll find a drum for Darren."

A little later a deafening noise came from Bertie's room. Eugene screeched on his violin while Darren bashed a biscuit tin with two wooden spoons. Bertie yelled out the words, sometimes breaking off to play a solo on his kazoo.

"*Jingle bells, jingle bells…*

Doo doo doo doo-doo

Oh what fun it is to…"

The door flew open. Bertie's dad stood there glaring.

"What's all the noise?" he demanded.

"We're practising," said Bertie. "Did you like it?"

"Like it? It sounds like someone's being murdered!" said Dad. "You've even driven Whiffer out of the house."

Bertie waved his kazoo. "We've got to practise," he said.

"What for?" asked Dad.

"So we can go busking," Bertie replied.

"You need a licence to go busking," said Dad. "Now please, pack it in. I'm trying to work."

He slammed the door.

Bertie's kazoo dribbled spit down his jumper. *Typical*, he thought. His parents went on and on at him to learn an instrument and when he did, they just complained!

CHAPTER 3

Darren and Eugene stayed for lunch.

"Mum, can we go busking this afternoon?" Bertie asked, sitting down at the table.

"Certainly not," said Mum. "We've been over this already."

"Pleeeease!" begged Bertie. "Not in town, just at the shops down the road."

"No, you're too young!" said Mum.

Darren reached for some crisps. "Bertie reckons we could make a fortune," he said.

"Does he now?" said Mum. "Well, he can dream on because you're not going."

Bertie threw back his head in despair. It was so unfair! All that practising for nothing! If they couldn't go busking, they might as well give up and go to the park. *Wait a minute*, thought Bertie. The park was on the way to the shops – and if they happened to take their instruments, who was going to know?

After lunch, they crept downstairs and tiptoed to the door.

"BERTIE!" called Mum. "Where do you think you're going?"

Uh-oh.

Dirty Bertie

"Just to the park!" Bertie shouted.

Mum came into the hall.

"Why are you all wearing your coats?"
she asked.

"It's cold!" said Bertie.

"It's the middle of June!" said Mum.

"Yes, but we need them for
goalposts," said Darren, thinking quickly.

The others nodded in agreement.

Mum narrowed her eyes.

Dirty Bertie

"Okay," she said. "But make sure you're back by four."

The three of them hurried out of the front door. Once they were down the road, they unzipped their coats. Eugene brought out his violin, and a biscuit tin and some spoons fell out of Darren's jacket. Bertie took his kazoo from his pocket.

"We made it," he said. "Let's get down the shops before anyone sees us."

Dirty Bertie

It was a bright summer's day and the local high street was busy. At the coffee shop customers sat outside, enjoying the sunshine. All was calm and peaceful.

Eugene fiddled nervously with his violin bow. He'd never played in public before.

"Can't we go somewhere a bit less busy?" he asked.

"No, this is perfect," said Bertie.

"If we see anyone we know, I'm not doing it," warned Darren.

"Stop worrying, it'll be fine!" said Bertie. "Who's got the hat?"

Eugene pulled a woolly hat from his pocket.

"We'll start over there," said Bertie, pointing to the café.

Dirty Bertie

They chose a spot close by and placed the hat on the ground. The buskers could only play three songs and Bertie didn't know all the words, but he doubted that anyone would notice.

"Ready?" he said. "One, two, three…"

"Twinkle twinkle, little star,
How I … doo-doo doo-doo dooo!"

Outside the café people looked up, startled. One minute they were enjoying the peace and quiet, the next it was shattered by three scruffy children making a terrible din. Some of the customers covered their ears. A baby in a buggy started to howl.

"What a row!" moaned the mother, rocking the buggy back and forth. "Please, somebody make them stop!"

A door banged
open and the
café manager
stormed out.

"What
do you think
you're doing?" he
demanded.

"Busking," said
Bertie. "It's like music on the street."

"I know what it is, but you can't do it
here," snapped the manager. "Clear off!"

He waved an arm at them and went
back inside.

Bertie frowned. He had expected a
bit more enthusiasm.

"Come on, let's go to the park,"
suggested Eugene, relieved.

"At least we gave it a try," said Darren.

Dirty Bertie

"But we haven't earned any money yet!" protested Bertie.

"You heard him. The manager told us to clear off!" said Darren.

Bertie looked at their audience. Maybe they'd started with the wrong song?

"Let's play 'Jingle Bells'," he suggested. "Everyone likes that. It makes you think of Christmas."

"But it's summer," said Eugene. The trouble with Bertie was he never knew when to give up.

"Jingle bells, jingle bells!
Doo doo, doo doo-doo!"

People at the café finished their drinks and left in a hurry.

"Oh what fun it is to ride…"

"STOP!" yelled the manager.

Dirty Bertie

The music stumbled to a halt.

"What did I tell you?" cried the manager. "You're driving all my customers away!"

Bertie looked around. The café did seem a little emptier than when they'd first arrived.

"Shall we play something else?" he asked.

"NO!" said the manager. "Just go! Find someone else to annoy!"

Bertie sighed and picked up the woolly hat. He held it out.

"I don't suppose you've got any spare change?"

CHAPTER 4

Further down the street, the three of them sat down on a bench.

"It's not fair!" grumbled Bertie. "We haven't earned a single penny."

"I told you we were wasting our time," said Eugene. "We might as well give up and go to the park."

But Bertie didn't admit defeat so easily.

Dirty Bertie

They were just starting to get the hang of busking.

On the square in front of them, children were running around while people sat on benches in the sun. It looked like an ideal spot for busking.

"Let's set up here," said Bertie.

The other two groaned.

"Face it, Bertie, this is never going to work!" said Darren.

"Just one last try, then we'll call it a day," promised Bertie.

They picked up their instruments again.

Bertie wiped the dribble off his kazoo and counted them in.

"One, two, three…"

Dirty Bertie

BOOM, CHIKKA, BOOM!

Bertie looked up. Across the square was the busker he'd seen in town earlier. His drum machine blared out as he began playing the saxophone.

"He can't do that!" complained Bertie. "This is our spot."

"But he can actually play," said Eugene.

"Maybe," said Bertie. "But there's three of us. I bet we can play louder!"

They launched into the last song on their playlist:

"The wheels on the bus go…"

BASH, BASH, BASH!

Darren thumped his drum.

"HEY!"

The busker had turned off his drum machine. He marched across the square towards them.

Dirty Bertie

"You again!" he said to Bertie. "What do you think you're playing at?"

"'The Wheels on the Bus'," replied Bertie.

"Well, cut it out! This is my pitch, find your own," snapped the busker.

He stomped back to his place, switched on the drum machine and began again.

Bertie stared. "What a cheek! We were here first!" he grumbled.

"We can't compete with that," said Darren. "It's proper music!"

"*Please*, let's just go to the park!" begged Eugene.

Dirty Bertie

But Bertie certainly wasn't giving up without a fight. Why should *they* be the ones to leave? If anyone should go, it was the busker – he was trying to pinch their audience!

"Start again and play louder," said Bertie.

They began playing. The busker glared and turned up his drum machine to full volume. Bertie yelled even louder to try and drown him out.

"THE HORN ON THE BUS GOES BEEP BEEP BEEP!"

Eugene's violin screeched. Darren bashed the biscuit tin so hard he put a dent in it. People around the square grabbed their children and fled to get away from the noise.

"OKAY, STOP! STOP!"

Dirty Bertie

The busker was back, waving his arms in front of them.

"I thought I told you to beat it!" he said.

"We were here first," replied Bertie.

"You were not!"

"We were so!"

"Look, you're just kids," said the busker. "I do this for a living. Why don't you just run along home, eh?"

Bertie folded his arms stubbornly.

The busker looked around. He was losing his audience fast.

"I'll give you a pound," he said, in desperation.

Bertie raised his eyebrows. "You mean a pound each?" he asked.

"No! Oh, all right, if you promise to clear off and never come back," said the busker.

Three pounds! It wasn't a fortune, but it was better than nothing.

"Come on, let's go to the sweet shop," said Darren.

They set off back along the street, but just as they reached the sweet shop,

Dirty Bertie

Bertie heard a voice he knew.

"BERTIE!"

Oh no – his mum and Suzy! Hadn't they done enough shopping for one day?

Mum spotted their instruments before they could hide them. She glared. "I thought you were going to the park?"

"We were…" said Bertie weakly.

"And what have you got there?" demanded Mum.

Bertie opened his hand to reveal the three pound coins.

"So despite everything I said, you went busking," said Mum. "I'll take the money, thank you. We'll give it to someone who deserves it."

They watched as she marched off down the street and stopped at the busker playing the saxophone. She

Dirty Bertie

dropped the coins into his hat.

Bertie put his head in his hands.

"*Now* can we go to the park?" groaned Eugene.

ROCKY!

CHAPTER 1

"Come on, everybody up! The sun's
shining!" cried Dad, throwing open the
curtains.

Mum groaned. Suzy hid under her
duvet. Bertie sat up and blinked. *Where
am I?* he thought. *This isn't my bedroom!*
Then he remembered – they were
staying in a youth hostel. Dad had

dragged them away for a weekend in the middle of nowhere.

"It's a beautiful day and we're surrounded by nature," said Dad. "Look out there – hills, trees, sheep!"

Bertie yawned. He'd seen sheep before and they had trees in the local park.

"We're not going on a *walk*, are we?" groaned Suzy.

"Better than that," said Dad. "We're going on an adventure!"

Bertie's eyes lit up. "You mean you're taking us to GO WILD!" he said.

He'd seen a poster for Go Wild! in the entrance hall. They had walkways and rope bridges, and you could swoop through the treetops on a zip wire like Tarzan. It looked amazing!

"Who needs theme parks?" said Dad.
"We've got all the thrills we need right
here. We're going to climb Craggy Peak!"

"Craggy what?" asked Suzy.

"Craggy Peak – it's a mountain," Dad
explained.

"You're not serious!" said Mum. "Surely
we should stick to climbing hills?"

"Bertie can't even climb a tree!"
hooted Suzy.

71

Dirty Bertie

"I can!" cried Bertie. He was brilliant at climbing trees, although getting down again was another matter.

"Don't worry," said Dad. "Anyone can climb Craggy Peak. There's an easy path that takes you right to the top."

"It's still a mountain," argued Mum. "What about the children?"

"It'll be good for them," said Dad.

"But we don't have the right gear," grumbled Suzy.

"Ah, that's where you're wrong," said Dad. He pulled out a large orange rucksack from under the bed. "I've brought everything we need. I've been planning this as a surprise!"

Bertie rolled his eyes. If his dad really wanted to surprise them, why didn't he take them to Disneyland?

Dirty Bertie

"What's the point of climbing a mountain?" he moaned.

"To get to the top, of course!" replied Dad. "Think of it as an adventure. We'll be like Scott of the Antarctic!"

"Isn't he the one that never came back?" said Mum grimly.

CHAPTER 2

Dad pulled into the car park and everyone climbed out.

"There it is!" cried Dad. "Craggy Peak!"

Bertie stared. Beyond the fields was a huge grey mountain. It was so high the peak was hidden in mist.

"We're not climbing that!" he groaned.

Dirty Bertie

"It'll be fun," said Dad. "Just think, you'll be able to tell your friends that you've actually climbed a mountain!"

Bertie thought he'd rather tell his friends that he'd actually been to Go Wild!

Dad opened the boot and hauled out the rucksack, staggering under its weight.

"What have you *got* in there?" asked Mum.

"Like I said, everything we need," replied Dad. "Maps, compass, hats, gloves, waterproofs, first-aid kit and plenty of water."

Dirty Bertie

"No biscuits?" asked Bertie.

Dad shook his head. "We've got a packed lunch from the youth hostel. Sandwiches, apples and energy bars."

Bertie plunged his hands in his pockets. They'd probably starve to death! Who in their right mind climbed a mountain without a packet of biscuits?

Mum was gazing up at Craggy Peak. "Are you sure about this?" she asked Dad. "What if the weather changes? And besides, should *you* be going up a mountain?"

"Me? I'm fine!" said Dad. "I can't wait to get going!"

He heaved the rucksack on to his back and got out the map.

"Okay, troops, forward march!" he cried.

They climbed over a stile to reach a muddy track winding uphill.

"Race you to the top!" cried Suzy.

"Last one's a smelly slug," said Bertie.

"DON'T RUN! Save your energy!" warned Dad. But Bertie and Suzy were already racing on ahead.

Dirty Bertie

An hour later they stopped by a stone wall. Dad took off the rucksack and dumped it on the ground.

"I need a rest!" he groaned, sitting on a tree stump.

"Already?" said Bertie. "I'm not even tired!"

Mountain climbing was turning out to be more fun than he'd expected. He'd already jumped in some sheep poo and sunk up to his ankles in a muddy bog.

Dirty Bertie

He'd even found a good poking stick that was great for annoying Suzy. All in all, things were looking up!

Mum and Dad, on the other hand, looked worn out. They were both sweating and red in the face. Dad kept grumbling that his new boots hurt and the rucksack weighed a ton.

"Are we nearly there?" asked Bertie. He'd lost sight of the mountain top.

"Not yet," said Dad.

He studied the map for a moment, frowning. He tried turning it the other way up.

"Hmm. Uh-huh. Mmm," he mumbled.

"We're not lost, are we?" asked Mum anxiously.

"Lost? Of course not!" snorted Dad. "It's just a case of finding the right path."

"Where *is* the right path?" asked Suzy.

They had been following a path, but
a while back it had divided into two.
Dad had decided the left path was right
(which sounded wrong). Now there was
no sign of any path at all.

"It must be straight on," Dad said,
folding the map.

Dirty Bertie

"*Up there?*" asked Mum. The rocks and boulders above looked gigantic.

"The path must be overgrown. I'm sure we'll find it," said Dad.

Mum glanced at the sky. "It looks like rain," she muttered. "That's all we need."

"Can I run on ahead and climb the rocks?" pleaded Bertie.

"No, stay with us," said Dad. "I don't want you getting into trouble."

Bertie sighed. He didn't see how he could get into any trouble. They were on a mountain in the middle of nowhere – what could possibly happen?

CHAPTER 3

The sky had grown darker. The wind beat against them as they clambered over the rocks. Bertie was out in front and hauled himself up. If this was the path, it was obviously made for mountain goats! Not that he minded. Climbing Craggy Peak was more exciting than he'd expected. Bertie imagined he

Dirty Bertie

was a famous explorer trekking through snow and watching out for polar bears. He stopped to wait for the others. After a few minutes, Suzy and Mum appeared.

"This is fun!" said Bertie.

"You think so?" panted Mum.

"It's an adventure!" said Bertie. "Are we climbing those massive rocks up there?"

Mum squinted at them and frowned.

"This can't be right," she said. "And where's your dad got to?"

"I thought he was with you," said Bertie.

They all looked round. A moment later a voice reached them, echoing from below.

"HEEEEEEEELP!"

Mum groaned. "I knew this would happen!" she said.

"What? He hasn't lost the sandwiches, has he?" asked Bertie.

"No," said Mum. "We'd better go back and help."

They found Dad further down on the rocks. He was standing on a narrow ledge, gripping the rock he was facing. He seemed to be hanging on for dear life, even though the drop below was only a couple of metres.

"You all right, Dad?" asked Bertie,

Dirty Bertie

looking down on him.

"Do I look all right? I CAN'T MOVE!" moaned Dad.

"Yes, you can," said Bertie. "You just have to let go of the rock."

"I CAN'T!" wailed Dad. "I'll fall!"

Bertie and Suzy looked puzzled.

"He's got vertigo," explained Mum. "He's scared of heights. Don't you remember the time he went on the big wheel at the funfair?"

Bertie had forgotten. Dad had kept his eyes shut the whole time.

"I warned you," said Mum. "I said this was a bad idea."

Dirty Bertie

"Never mind that, just get me down!" cried Dad.

Bertie couldn't see what Dad was making such a fuss about. He climbed down to the ledge, treading on his hand.

"OWW!" howled Dad.

"Give me your hand, I can pull you up," said Bertie.

Dad shook his head. There was no way he was letting go of the rock. He needed both hands to hang on.

"I know, what if Mum gives you a piggyback?" suggested Bertie.

Dirty Bertie

Suzy gave him a withering look. "Can't we just go back down?" she asked.

"NO! That's even worse!" said Dad.

"Well, what do you want us to do?" asked Mum. "We can't stay here forever!"

Dad shook his head helplessly.

"If we're stopping, can we have our sandwiches?" asked Bertie.

"NO!" shouted everyone at once.

Bertie shrugged. He was only asking. There was no point in going hungry.

Mum tried to ring the youth hostel on her mobile, but there was no signal. Someone would have to go and get help.

"Suzy, you and Bertie go back down while I stay here with Dad," she said.

"I don't mind staying!" offered Bertie. After all, the food was in Dad's rucksack.

"No, you go with Suzy," ordered Mum. "As soon as you find someone, explain to them what's happened. And be careful!"

"Okay!" sighed Bertie. "*Then* can we have lunch?"

No one answered. Everyone seemed to be in a bad mood. He sighed. This never would have happened if they'd gone to Go Wild! It was difficult to get stuck if you were whizzing down a zip wire.

CHAPTER 4

Bertie followed Suzy as they made their way back down the mountain. Before long they reached the stone wall where they had rested coming up. Further on, they came to the spot where the paths divided. Bertie spotted a group of ramblers coming up the slope.

"Leave the talking to me," said Suzy as

they went to meet them.

"Excuse me!" she said. "Our dad's back there and he's got sort of stuck."

"Oh dear!" said one of the women. "Where is he?"

"On the rocks! He's hanging on by his fingernails!" said Bertie dramatically.

Suzy glared at him to shut up. "He's stuck on a sort of ledge," she said. "But we can't get him to move."

"Mum says he's got lurgy toes!" added Bertie.

"Good heavens!" gasped the woman.

Suzy sighed. "He means vertigo. But we're not sure what to do – Mum sent us to get help."

"Is he in any danger?" asked one of the men.

"Well, not really," said Suzy.

Dirty Bertie

"He could be," said Bertie. "His legs have gone wobbly so he could fall."

The ramblers looked alarmed. The woman took out her phone.

"I think we'd better call Mountain Rescue," she said. "They'll know what to do. Let's see if I can get a signal."

Mountain Rescue? Bertie thought that sounded fantastic. He didn't even know there *was* a Mountain Rescue!

Bertie and Suzy climbed back up the mountain to their parents.

"Help's on the way," said Suzy.

Half an hour later they heard a loud whirring noise overhead. A blast of wind kicked up the dust. Dad looked up in surprise.

"Oh, you're kidding!" he groaned.

"Why have they sent a helicopter?" cried Mum.

"You told us to get help!" said Bertie.

"Yes, but I didn't mean Mountain Rescue!" said Mum. "Your dad's just scared of heights."

"It's not my fault," said Suzy. "It was

Bertie. He made it sound as if Dad was hanging off a cliff!"

Bertie couldn't see why they were complaining. They'd asked for help and what could be better than Mountain Rescue? Besides, he'd always wanted to go in a helicopter!

The rescue team jumped out. They climbed down to the ledge, bringing ropes, a stretcher and a first-aid kit.

"Are you hurt?" asked the team leader. "Did you fall?"

Dad shook his head.

"Any broken bones?"

"I don't think so," muttered Dad.

"So what's the problem?" asked the woman.

Dad had gone bright pink. He mumbled something about getting stuck.

Dirty Bertie

"He's scared of heights," Mum explained. "He gets vertigo."

"I see," said the team leader. "Maybe you should have thought of that before you climbed a mountain."

They strapped Dad on to the stretcher since he was too shaky to walk. Then the rescue team hauled him up off the ledge and carried him to the helicopter. Mum, Suzy and Bertie followed behind.

"Well, are you coming with us?" asked the rescue team leader.

"Wicked!" said Bertie, peering inside. "Can I sit at the front?"

With a whirr of blades the helicopter lifted into the sky. Bertie was given some sweet tea and a biscuit. He gazed down as they pulled away from the mountain. Wait till he told Darren and

Eugene about this!

Minutes later he could see rows of tiny cars in the car park. Further on he spotted a wood with rope bridges, walkways and zip wires. Bertie pointed excitedly.

"Look, there's Go Wild! Can we go tomorrow?" he begged. "Can we, pleeeease?"

Mum groaned. "ANYTHING!" she said. "Just as long as it doesn't involve mountains."